AT THE DENTIST

What Did Christopher See?

By Sandra Ziegler

Illustrated by
Mina Gow McLean

THE CHILD'S WORLD

ELGIN, ILLINOIS 60120

Distributed by Childrens Press, 1224 West Van Buren Street,
Chicago, Illinois 60607.

Library of Congress Cataloging in Publication Data

Ziegler, Sandra, 1938-
  At the dentist — what did Christopher see?

  (Going places)
  SUMMARY: A young boy creates Mr. Plaque, Sir Sweet,
Ms. Toothbrush, and Mr. Floss after he and his sister
visit the dentist and learn about tooth care.
  [1. Dental care—Fiction. 2. Teeth—Care and
hygiene—Fiction] I. McLean, Mina Gow. II. Title.
PZ7.Z495As   [E]   76-18960
ISBN 0-913778-63-X

Christopher Allen Sangree gave his cactus a little water and sat back on his heels to admire it. His cactus looked beautiful in the special pot his grand-mother had made him. He grinned, thinking about his grandmother.

3

Christopher's mother put the receiver back on the telephone. "Tomorrow, Karina will make her first visit to the dentist," she said. "Dr. Thompson's office just called to remind me that both of you have appointments."

"Oh," moaned Christopher. He made a face.

"Now don't do that," said Mother. "You know going to the dentist is not that bad. You don't want to frighten Karina, do you?"

"No," agreed Christopher. "Has the dentist moved into his new office yet?"

"Yes," said Mother. "Last month."

The next day, when Mother opened the door with the dentist's name on it, Christopher walked right in. But Karina did not budge.

"Look, Karina," said Christopher. "Do you want to see the gerbils?" Dr. Thompson kept a cage of gerbils in his waiting room just so children could watch the gerbils while they waited.

Karina could not resist the urge to look. Besides, everything in that room seemed friendly enough.

Mother stopped at the window to let Ms. Cantwell know they were there.

"Hello, Christopher," said the dentist as Christopher came into the examining room. "Are you having any trouble with your teeth?"

"They are falling out," said Christopher, grinning to show his missing tooth.

Dr. Thompson laughed. "Glad to hear it," he said. "That is just what those teeth ought to do. We will take good care of the next set to be sure they don't fall out."

"You must be Karina," the dentist said, smiling at her too. Karina snuggled closer to her mother's knee.

Dr. Thompson's new office was not at all like his old one, but Dr. Thompson showed Christopher that everything he needed was right there in the bright cabinet — that is, everything but the X-ray machine. It was separate. Somehow, the cheerful color it wore made Christopher want to smile for a picture.

"Does your chair still move?" asked Christopher.

"It still does," Dr. Thompson answered. "Let's put Karina in it and give her a ride."

After the ride up, Karina hung on to Mother's hand and bravely opened her mouth. Dr. Thompson checked her teeth with the silver toothpick that Christopher remembered.

"Not a single cavity," said Dr. Thompson. "You have good, strong teeth, Karina."

"Teeth have two enemies," Dr. Thompson continued as he gave Karina a ride down in the big chair. "Plaque and sweets."

"What is plaque?" asked Christopher.

"Plaque," explained the dentist, "is something you cannot see that sticks to your teeth. It is made of tiny food particles and plants called bacteria. When you eat something sweet and don't brush your teeth, the sugar feeds the plaque. The combination makes an acid. The acid eats into the tooth and makes a cavity."

"No wonder brushing is so important," said Christopher. He imagined a funny picture in his mind, and he called it Mr. Plaque.

"Yes," said the dentist. "And if you cannot brush, you should at least rinse your mouth after you eat."

Dr. Thompson held up his dental mirror. "You can take better care of your teeth if you have a mouth mirror. I will show you how."

He handed Mother some disclosing tablets. "Let Christopher and Karina each chew a tablet before they brush their teeth; then let them rinse a little water in their mouths and spit it out before they look in the mirror."

"I know what I will see," said Christopher. He had done this before. "I'll see red teeth."

"Right," said the dentist. "With a mouth mirror and a regular mirror, you can see all your teeth on both sides. Where you see red, you must brush better."

Dr. Thompson handed Karina and Christopher new toothbrushes. He handed Mother a sample of unwaxed dental floss and a plastic floss holder.

"My assistant will show the children how to brush and floss," said Dr. Thompson. "They should brush and floss every night before they go to bed. You will have to help Karina."

Christopher climbed into the chair to have his teeth examined and then cleaned. As Dr. Thompson worked on his teeth, Christopher studied the picture on the wall in front of him.

When the dentist took his hands out of Christopher's mouth so he could talk, Christopher said, "I'm going to learn how to do that."

"What?" asked Dr. Thompson.

Christopher pointed to the picture.

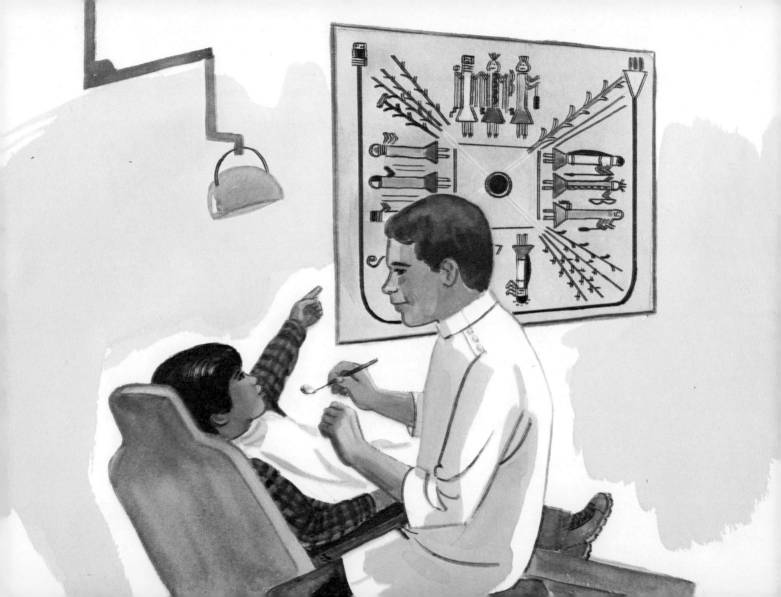

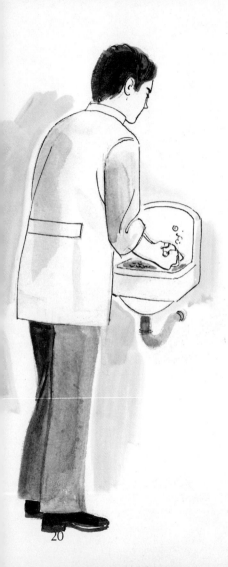

"Navaho sand painting?" asked Dr. Thompson.

"Yes," answered Christopher. "In my craft class."

When the dentist was finished, Christopher walked over to examine the picture more closely. He knew that everything in a sand painting meant something, but mostly he just liked to look at the charming characters.

Dr. Thompson told his two patients good-bye. "Watch those between-meal snacks," he said. "And I'll see you in six months."

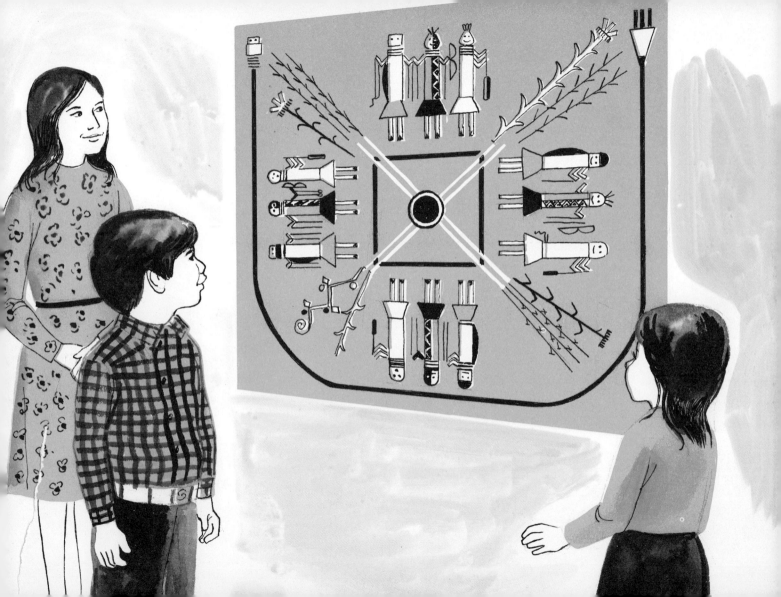

"May I paint for awhile?" Christopher asked as Mother drove the car into the garage.

"I want to brush my teeth," said Karina as she touched the comical dog on her new toothbrush holder.

"Karina, you may do that right now," said Mother. "And, yes, Christopher, you may paint."

22

Christopher knew just what he wanted to make — some things he had seen in his imagination while at the dentist's office. And he would make them like the sand pictures — only he would use paint. He chose some big sheets of paper for his easel, got out several colors of paint and some brushes, and was soon busily at work.

Early one evening a few nights later, Christopher came into the living room. "Everybody come to my art exhibit," he said.

Mother was busy at the loom in the corner making a special design in a rug for Karina's room, for Mother truly liked to weave. She was not sure she wanted to stop.

Father put down his book. "All right," he agreed, so Mother went along too.

"What do we have here?" asked Father as he looked at two of Christopher's paintings.

"Mr. Plaque," said Christopher, "and Sir Sweet."

"Who are they?" asked Father.

"Enemies," said Christopher. "Together they work to eat up your teeth."

Mr. Plaque

Sir Sweet

"And who are these two?" asked Father, stopping before two pictures on the other wall.

"That's a lady toothbrush," guessed Karina.

"Yes," said Christopher. "She is Ms. Toothbrush. We use her after every meal."

"This must be Floss," said Mother.

"Right," said Christopher. "Two friends my teeth need every day."

"With such good pictures to help me remember," said Father, "I am sure I won't forget what helps and what hurts my teeth."

Christopher smiled that special smile people smile when they feel good inside.